THE GIFT

A Magical Story about
Caring for the Earth

Wisdom Publications · Boston

Once upon a time there was a king and queen
who lived in a kingdom far away.
One day the king and queen heard about
a very wise man who lived in
a village of their kingdom.

The queen wanted to hear the advice of the wise man, so she invited him and his followers to visit the palace.

She spent a whole day listening to their wise advice and at the end she decided to give them a gift.

The wise man asked Ananda, his main follower, to receive the queen's gift.

The queen gave Ananda a big bag of gold. And all the wise men and the queen were very happy.

But when the king heard about his wife's gift,
he became very suspicious.
He thought that Ananda must have tricked
the queen into giving him the gold, so he called
Ananda in to question him.

" What are you going to do with so much money?"
the king asked.
"I will go to the market and buy all the cloth my
friends and I can carry," Ananda replied.

"And what are you going to do with all that cloth?"
"We will sew five hundred suits of clothes."

"What will you do with five
hundred suits of clothes?" the king asked.
"Your majesty," said Ananda, "many of the
people here go about dressed in rags.
I will give the new clothes to them."

"And what about their old clothes?" asked the king. "We will make them into quilts."

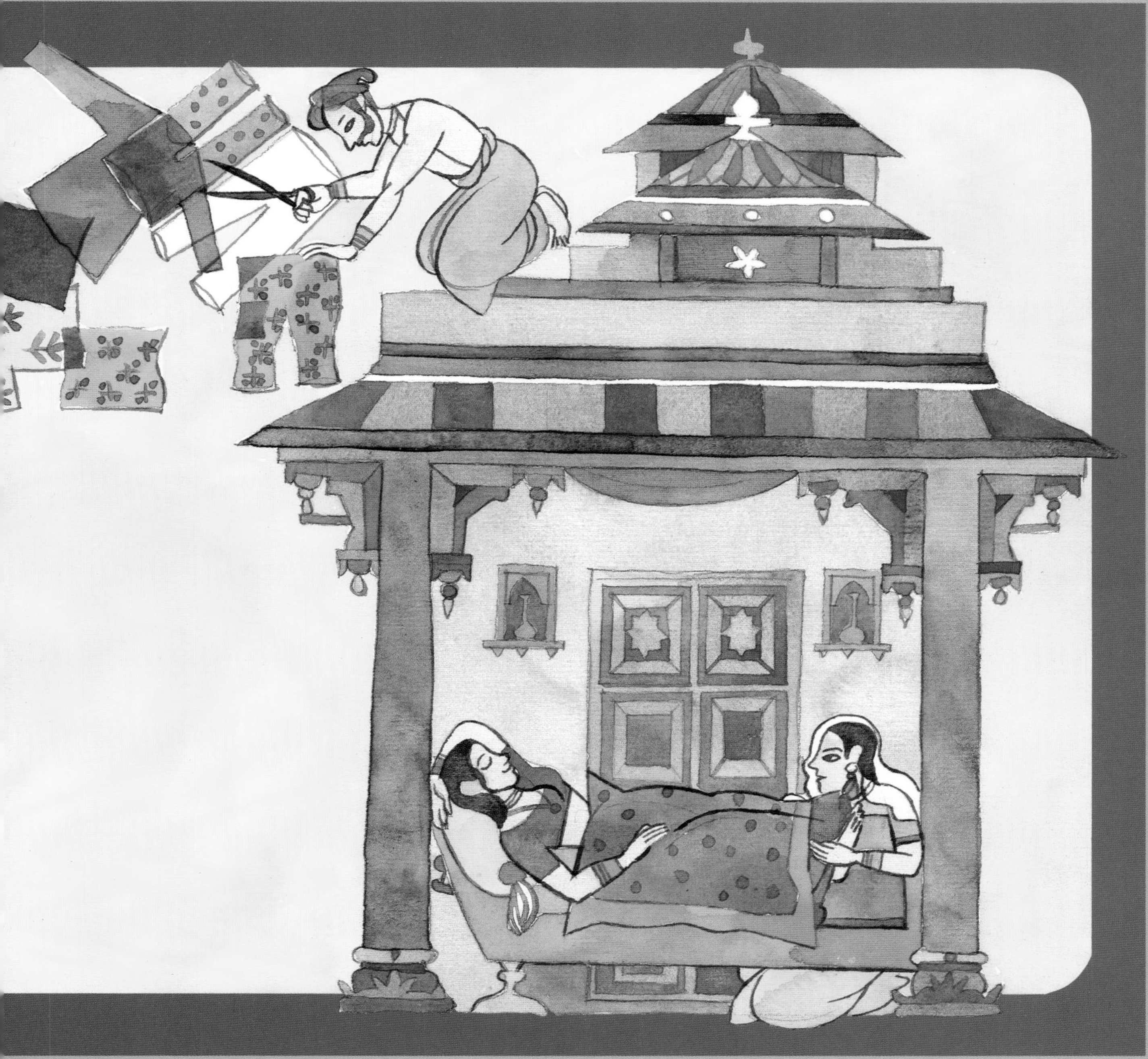

"And what about the old quilts?"
"We will make them into pillows."

"And what about the old pillows?"
"We will make them into rugs."

"And what about the old rugs?"
"We will make them into doormats."

"And what about the old doormats?"
"We will make them into brooms."

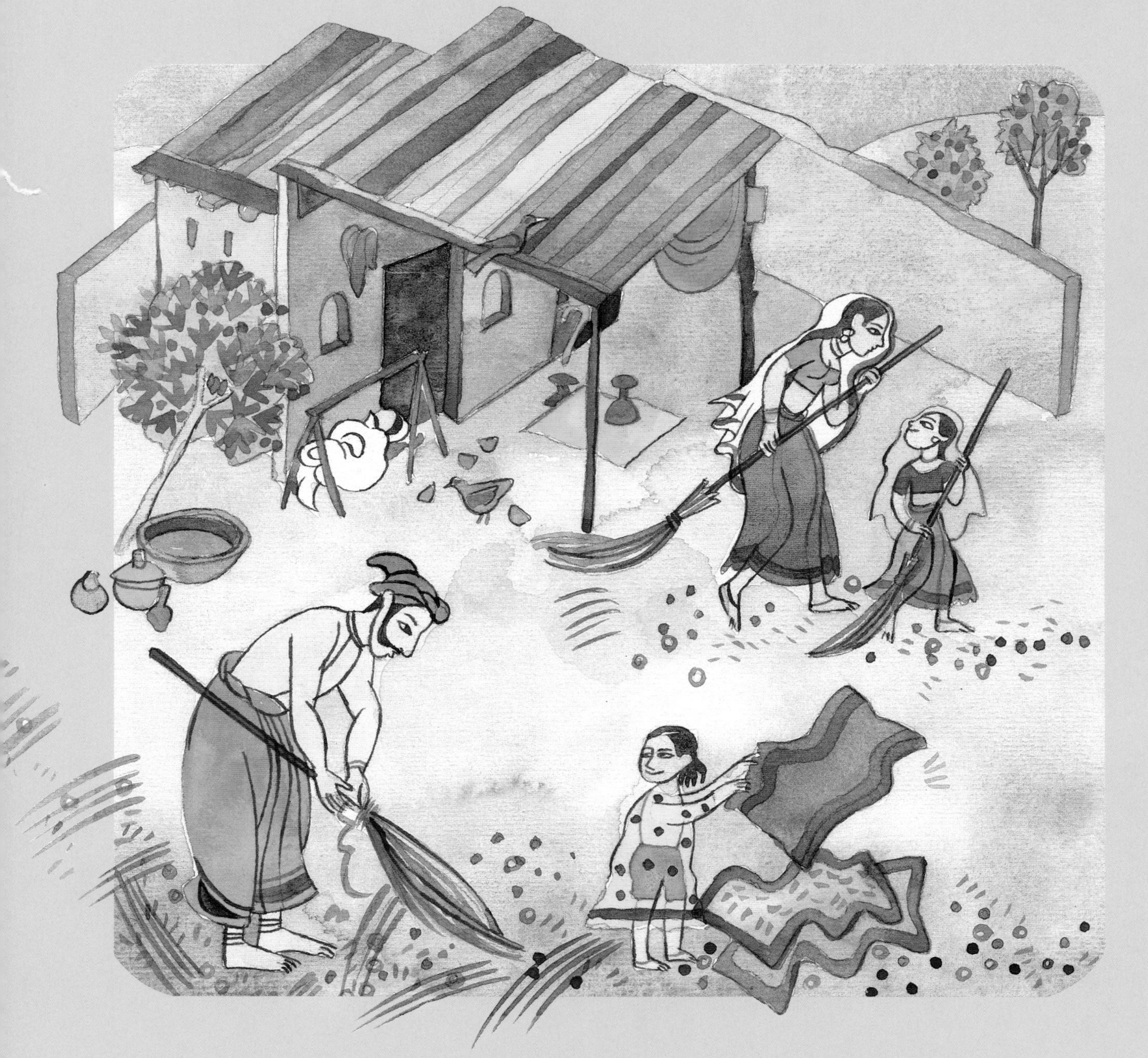

"And what about the old brooms?"
"Well, your majesty, we take them apart
and mix the bits with mud, and then we
use it to plaster the walls of our houses."

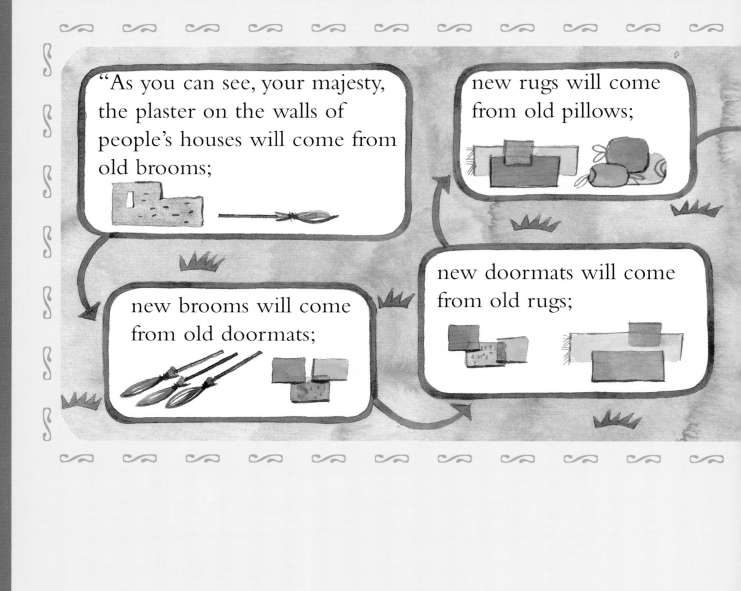

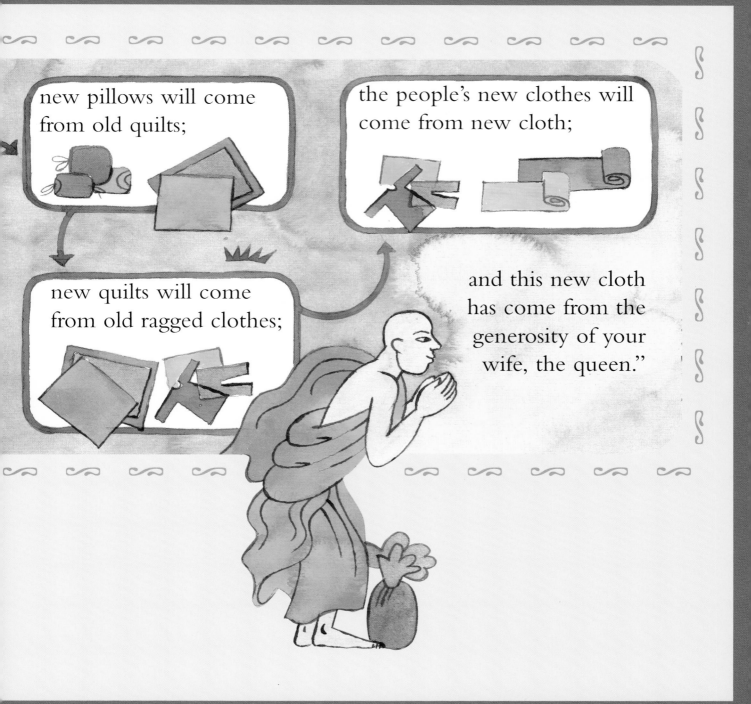

"In this way, your majesty, we learn that everything that comes to each of us must be used thoughtfully and with great care, for a useful purpose. Nothing is really 'ours' to own, since everything in the universe has been given to us as a gift merely to use for a little while. Gifts are to be shared. And we must always be mindful of this as we go through life."